AF506540

Eco-Chic Beauty:
A Guide to DIY Self Care

Natural Beauty and
Wellness Recipes

Eco-Chic Beauty: A Guide to DIY Self-Care

Mia Mirk

Published by Mia Mirk, 2024.

Mia Mirk

Copyright © 2024 by Mia Mirk.

All rights reserved.

No portion of this book may be reproduced in any form without written permission from the publisher or author, except as permitted by the Canadian copyright act.

This is a work of fiction. Similarities to real people, places, or events are entirely coincidental.

ECO-CHIC BEAUTY: A GUIDE TO DIY SELF-CARE

First edition. August 29, 2024.

Copyright © 2024 Mia Mirk.

ISBN: 979-8227999160

Written by Mia Mirk.

In today's fast-paced and hectic world, prioritizing self-care and wellness has become increasingly essential. This book serves as a gateway to the world of do-it-yourself (DIY) beauty and wellness, inviting readers to embark on a journey of holistic self-care using natural and nourishing ingredients. It provides an overview of the significance of DIY beauty and wellness practices, the benefits they offer, and the empowering experience of creating one's own natural self-care products. Readers will discover the joy of creating their own all-natural beauty and wellness products, allowing for a deeper connection with self-care rituals and a more conscious approach to personal well-being. Each recipe is accompanied by an in-depth explanation of the ingredients used and their specific benefits, making it a valuable resource for those

seeking to enhance their natural beauty and wellness journey. This comprehensive guide provides a wide array of DIY beauty and wellness recipes using natural and nourishing ingredients. From soothing face masks to invigorating body scrubs, these recipes are designed to promote self-care, relaxation, and overall well-being. Each recipe is thoughtfully crafted to harness the benefits of natural elements, such as botanical extracts, essential oils, and wholesome pantry staples. The step-by-step instructions make it easy for readers to create their own spa-like experiences at home, where they can indulge in natural beauty practices for the skin, hair, and overall wellness.

Table of contents

Part one: *The benefits of natural ingredients; the does and don'ts:*

- Physical benefits of using natural ingredient... P.12
- Mental and emotional benefits of using natural ingredients...P.14
- Things to keep in mind when making DIY health and beauty recipes... P.16
- Benefits of opting for organic ingredients... P.21
- Things to avoid when making DIY health and beauty recipes...P.24

Part Two: *The recipes*

- 1. Hydrating Honey and Oatmeal Face mask...P.27
- 2. Energizing Citrus Body Scrub...P.29
- 3. Nourishing Avocado Hair Mask...P.31
- 4. Calming Lavender and Chamomile Bath Soak...P.33
- 5. Refreshing Cucumber and Mint Cooling Mist.P.36
- 6. Soothing Aloe Vera and Green Tea Eye Gel...P.38
- 7. Revitalizing Rose and Coconut Bath Bombs...P.40

- 8. Balancing Yogurt and Turmeric Face Cleanser...P.42
- 9. Glow Boosting Pineapple and Papaya Enzyme Mask...P.44
- 10. Herbal Hair Rinse for Shine and Scalp Health....P.46
- 11. Soothing Coconut and Shea Butter Body Lotion...P.48
- 12. Eucalyptus And Peppermint Foot Soak...P.50
- 13. Acne-Fighting Tea Tree and Witch Hazel Toner...P.52
- 14. Turmeric and Honey Brightening Face Scrub...P.54
- 15. Calendula and Rose Infused Facial Steam...P.56
- 16. Soothing Aloe and Lavender After-Sun Gel...P.58
- 17. Rosemary and Mint Scalp Scrub...P.60
- 18. Green Tea and Honey Face Mask for Rejuvenation...P.62
- 19. Vanilla and Lavender Relaxing Bath Salts...P.64
- 20. Coconut Oil and Coffee Under Eye Dark Circle Treatment...P.67
- 21. Castor oil and Aloe Vera Hair Thickening Mask...P.69
- 22. Nail Strengthening Oil...P.71
- 23. Clarifying Shampoo...P.74
- 24. Coconut and Aloe Vera Hair Conditioner...P.77
- 25. Coconut Oil and Shea Butter Cleansing Balm...P.80
- 26. Anti-Aging Face Cream...P.83
- 27. Soothing Face Cream for Rosacea...P.86

- 28. Clarifying and nourishing makeup remover...P.88
- 29. Coco and Cinnamon foundation powder...P.91
- 30. Lemon and Honey Hair Brightening Treatment...P.94
- Meet the Author...P.97

Part One

Physical benefits of using natural ingredients

Nourishing yourself with natural ingredients can have significant physical and mental benefits. Let's dive into the physical benefits:

- Nutrient Density: Natural ingredients, such as fruits, vegetables, and whole grains, are rich in essential nutrients, including vitamins, minerals, and antioxidants. These nutrients are crucial for supporting various bodily functions, such as immune function, energy production, and tissue repair.

- Digestive Health: Many natural ingredients, such as fiber-rich vegetables and whole grains, support digestive health by promoting regular bowel movements and fostering a healthy gut microbiome. A healthy gut microbiome is linked to improved digestion, nutrient absorption, and overall well-being.

- Hydration and Fluid Balance: Natural ingredients like fruits and vegetables often have high water content, aiding in hydration. Proper hydration is vital for maintaining optimal bodily functions, including temperature regulation, joint lubrication, and waste removal.

- Healthy Fats and Proteins: Ingredients like avocados, nuts, seeds, and fish oils provide essential fatty acids and proteins that are crucial for cell structure, hormone production, brain function, and muscle repair.

- Reduced Toxin Exposure: Many natural ingredients are free from additives, preservatives, and synthetic chemicals, reducing the body's exposure to potentially harmful substances commonly found in processed foods and skincare products.

Mental and emotional benefits of using natural ingredients

Using natural ingredients can also be very beneficial for both our mental and emotional wellbeing. Some examples of this include:

- Mood Support: Certain natural ingredients contain compounds that may positively influence mood and mental well-being. For example, omega-3 fatty acids have been linked to lower rates of depression and improved cognitive function.

- Stress Reduction: Using nourishing natural foods can positively impact stress levels. Certain nutrients, such as magnesium can help regulate cortisol (the "stress hormone") levels, potentially reducing stress and anxiety.

- Reduction Of Chemical Exposure: choosing natural ingredients in health and beauty products can reduce exposure to synthetic chemicals, which may contribute to mental clarity and peace of mind.

• Nutrient- Rich: Natural ingredients are packed with vitamins, minerals, antioxidants, and essential fatty acids that nourish and rejuvenate the skin and hair from within.

• Holistic Wellness: natural ingredients often address multiple facets of wellbeing, encompassing physical, emotional, and spiritual aspects. The holistic approach can promote a sense of balance and overall wellness. These ingredients not only benefit your exterior but can also have therapeutic effects on your mind and body.

• Cost effective: Many ingredients are affordable and can often be found in your kitchen or garden. This makes DIY beauty recipes a cost effect alternative to expensive commercial products.

• Safety and Gentleness: Natural ingredients are generally gentler on the skin and hair compared to many commercial products that contain many chemicals, synthetic fragrances and preservatives. This makes them ideal for those with sensitive skin types.

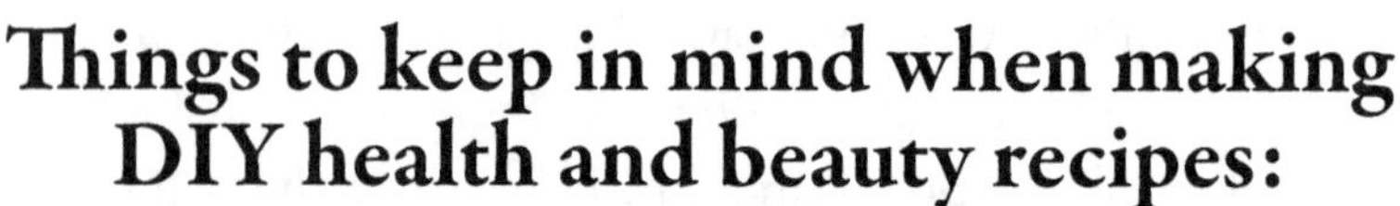

Things to keep in mind when making DIY health and beauty recipes:

When creating DIY health and beauty recipes, it's crucial to keep certain factors in mind to ensure safety, efficacy, and a positive experience. Here are some key considerations for crafting DIY recipes:

⬦ Allergies and Sensitivities:

> Patch test: Before applying any new ingredients or mixture to your skin or hair, do a patch test. Apply a small amount to a discreet area, like the inside or your wrist or behind your ear and wait 24 hours to see if there's any adverse reaction.

> Allergy awareness: be aware of common allergens like nuts, essential oils, and certain plans. Avoid ingredients that you know cause allergies or sensitivity.

⬦ Quality of Ingredients:

> Freshness: always use fresh ingredients. Spoiled or expired ingredients can cause skin irritations or infections.

> Purity: opt for organic and unprocessed ingredients whenever possible to avoid pesticides and other harmful chemicals

> Source: purchased from reputable sources to ensure the authenticity and quality of the ingredients.

◇ Hygiene and Cleanliness:

> Sterilize tools and containers: Ensure that all tools (mixing bowls, spoons, jars) are thoroughly cleaned and sterilized to prevent contamination.

> Personal Hygiene: Wash your hands before making any DIY recipes to avoid introducing bacteria into your formulations.

◇ Storage and Shelf life:

> Proper Storage: Store your DIY products in clean, airtight containers. Glass jars are often preferable to plastic as they do not leach chemicals.

> Refrigeration: Some DIY recipes, especially those with fresh ingredients like fruits or dairy, need to be stored in the refrigerator to prolong their shelf life.

> Short Shelf Life: Be mindful that natural products typically have a shorter shelf life than commercial products due to the absence of preservatives. Use them within a week or two, depending on the ingredients.

◈ Measurement and Consistency:

> Accurate Measurement: Follow recipes accurately to ensure the effectiveness and safety of the product. Improper ratio can lead to ineffective or harmful mixtures.

> Consistency: Keep track of what works for you. If you tweak a recipe, write down the changes so you can replicate successful results or adjust as needed.

◈ Understanding Ingredients:

> Research: Understand the properties and potential effects of each ingredient. Some natural ingredients can be potent and may cause irritation if used improperly.

> Complementary ingredients: Learn which ingredients work well together and which should be kept separate. For example, mixing acidic ingredients like lemon juice with baking soda can neutralize their effects.

◈ Essential Oils:

> Dilution: Essential oils are highly concentrated and should always be diluted with a carrier oil before application to the skin. Common carrier oils include coconut oil, jojoba oil, and almond oil.

> Usage limit: Stick to recommended usage levels of essential oils, typically a few drops per tablespoon or carrier oil.

◇ Personalization:

> Skin and Hair Type: Customize recipes based on your specific skin and hair type. For instance, oily skin might benefit from clay masks, while dry skin might need more hydrating ingredients like honey or aloe vera.

> Preference: Adjust scents and textures to suite your personal preferences and ensure a pleasant experience with your DIY products.

◇ Safety Precautions:

> Avoid Eye Area: Be cautious when applying products near the eyes. Some ingredients can cause irritation or damage to the eyes.

> Sun Sensitivity: Some ingredients, like citrus oils, can increase your skin's sensitivity to the sun. Avoid sun exposure after using such ingredients to apply them at night.

◇ Document and Experimentation:

> Keep a Journal: Document your recipes, include the ingredients used, proportions, and any adjustments made. Note the effects on your skin or hair to track what works best for you.

> Experiment wisely: Start with simple recipes and gradually experiment with more complex ones as you become more comfortable and knowledgeable about the ingredients and process.

Creating DIY Health and beauty recipes can be a delightful and beneficial practice, blending creativity and self-care. By keeping these considerations in mind, you can ensure that your homemade products are safe, effective and tailored to your unique needs. Enjoy the process and natural beauty that comes with it.

Benefits of opting for organic ingredients:

Opting for organic ingredients when making DIY health and beauty products can offer several important benefits:

• Reduced Exposure to Pesticides and Chemicals: Organic ingredients are cultivated without the use of synthetic pesticides, herbicides, and fertilizers. Choosing organic can minimize exposure to potentially harmful chemicals often found in conventionally grown plants.

• High Nutrient Content: Organic ingredients are often richer in nutrients such as vitamins, minerals, and antioxidants. The nutrient density of organic plants can contribute to the overall effectiveness of DIY health and beauty products.

• Support for Sustainable Practices: Organic farming practices prioritize environmental sustainability, including soil health, water conservation, and biodiversity. By choosing organic ingredients, consumers can support environmentally responsible practices.

• Avoidance of Genetically Modified Organisms (GMOs): Organic ingredients are non-GMO. Opting for organic can help individuals avoid ingredients derived from genetically modified crops, promoting a preference for natural and unaltered sources.

• Promotion of Animal Welfare: Certified organic ingredients are not tested on animals and are cultivated with standards that prioritize animal welfare. As such, choosing organic aligns with ethical considerations related to animal testing.

• Reduced Environmental Impact: Organic farming practices are often associated with a lower environmental impact due to reduced chemical usage and an emphasis on soil and ecosystem health. Opting for organic ingredients can contribute to more sustainable living.

• Minimized Allergen Exposure: Organic ingredients are typically grown and processed without common allergens, additives, or artificial flavors. This can be beneficial for individuals with sensitivities or allergies.

• Holistic Approach to Personal Care: Incorporating organic ingredients in DIY health and beauty products aligns with a holistic approach to personal care, promoting overall well-being and harmony with nature.

● Trust and Transparency: Certified organic products often undergo stringent regulations and certification processes, providing consumers with a level of trust and transparency regarding the origin and quality of the ingredients.

● Passion for Clean Living: For individuals who are passionate about clean living and ethical consumption, opting for organic ingredients reflects a commitment to natural, sustainable, and health conscious practices. Overall, choosing organic ingredients for DIY health and beauty products can contribute to a more sustainable, health-conscious, and environmentally responsible approach to self-care.

Things to avoid when making DIY health and beauty recipes:

When creating DIY health and beauty recipes, it's important to be mindful of potential pitfalls and to avoid certain practices to ensure safety and effectiveness. Here are some key things to avoid when making DIY health and beauty recipes:

- Unsafe or Unverified Ingredients: Avoid using ingredients that are unverified, have questionable sourcing, or lack evidence of safety and efficacy for topical use.

- Excessive Use of Essential Oils: Overuse of essential oils can lead to skin sensitization and irritation. Adhere to recommended dilution rates, and if in doubt, seek professional guidance.

- Harsh Abrasives in Exfoliants: Avoid using harsh or large exfoliating particles that can cause micro-tears in the skin, leading to irritation and sensitivity.

● Unhygienic Practices: Ensure all utensils, containers, and working surfaces are thoroughly cleaned and sanitized to prevent contamination and microbial growth in the products.

● Lack of Preservation in Water-Based Products: If formulating water-based products (e.g., toners or mists), consider the need for a natural preservative to prevent bacterial growth.

● Poor Storage Practices: Improper storage of DIY products can lead to spoilage and loss of efficacy. Be mindful of temperature and light exposure to preserve the integrity of the products.

● Overcomplicated Formulations: Avoid making overly complex recipes, especially when starting out. It's important to understand the interactions between different ingredients before formulating complex products.

● Absence of Patch Testing: Failing to conduct patch tests can lead to adverse reactions on a larger skin area. Always conduct a patch test when introducing a new ingredient or product.

● Misinformation and Pseudoscience: Be cautious of misinformation and pseudoscientific claims surrounding DIY health and beauty. Rely on credible sources and scientific evidence.

● Neglecting Individual Needs and Allergies: One size does not fit all in DIY health and beauty. Avoid neglecting individual skin types, allergies, and sensitivities when formulating products.

By being mindful of these potential pitfalls and avoiding these practices, it's possible to create safe, effective, and enjoyable DIY health and beauty products.

Incorporating natural ingredients into your DIY beaty recipes not only enhances your beauty regimen but also promotes a sustainable, cost-effective, and health-conscious lifestyle. By harnessing the power of nature, you can achieve glowing skin, and luscious hair while being kind to the earth and your body.

Part Two

1. Hydrating Honey and Oatmeal Face Mask

Ingredients:

- Oatmeal
- Honey
- Plain Yogurt
- Aloe Vera Gel

Benefits:

Oatmeal: is a gentle exfoliant that helps to remove dead skin cells, soothes irritation, and provides moisture to the skin. It contains beta-glucans, which have anti-inflammatory properties and can help with skin dryness and itching.

Honey: has natural antibacterial properties and is a humectant, which means it helps keep the skin hydrated and retains moisture. It also contains antioxidants that can help protect the skin from damage.

Plain Yogurt: is a gentle exfoliant, promoting a smoother and brighter complex. It also locks in moisture while hydrating the skin and can help balance the natural oils. May also combat acne causing bacteria.

Aloe Vera Gel: has a hydrating, soothing and cooling effect making it great for sensitive skin. It is also great for wound healing, inflammation, cuts and burns.

Combine:

- 1 tablespoon of Oatmeal
- 1 tablespoon of Honey
- 1 tablespoon of Plain Yogurt
- 1 teaspoon of Aloe Vera Gel

Instructions:

1. Clean face with your cleanser of choice. Make sure to always apply the mask on a freshly cleaned face.
2. Combine all the ingredients in a bowl.
3. Apply the face mask, avoiding the eyes.
4. Let the mask do its wonders for 10-15 minutes.
5. Rinse off with warm water, delicately dabbing your skin dry.
6. Repeat 1-2x a week.

2.Energizing Citrus Body Scrub

Ingredients:

- Sea Salt
- Coconut Oil
- Fresh Lemon Zest
- Orange Essential Oil

Benefits:

Sea Salt: is a natural exfoliant that helps remove dead skin cells, unclogs pores, and can help with conditions such as acne or eczema. It also contains minerals, such as magnesium and calcium.

Coconut Oil: is a rich source of fatty acids that can help moisturize and protect the skin's barrier function. It also has antimicrobial properties that may benefit skin health.

Fresh Lemon Zest: the natural fruit acids can help exfoliate and brighten the skin due to its Vitamin C and antioxidants. It also has antibacterial and antifungal properties. Can also help control excess oil, making it great for individuals with oily or acne skin.

Orange Essential Oil: has a bright, uplifting aroma and contains compounds that can help promote feelings of relaxation and well-being. It's often used in aromatherapy for its mood-boosting properties.

Combine:

- 1 cup of Sea Salt
- ¼ cup of melted Coconut Oil
- Lemon Zest of one Lemon
- 10-15 drops of Orange Essential Oil

Instructions:

1. Combine all the ingredients listed above in a bowl.
2. Thoroughly mix the ingredients to create a scrub.
3. While in the shower, gently massage the scrub onto your skin using circular motions, then rinse it off with warm water.

3.Nourishing Avocado Hair Mask

Ingredients:

- Avocado
- Egg
- Coconut Oil
- Honey

Benefits:

Avocado: is rich in healthy fats and antioxidants, such as vitamins E and C, which can help nourish and protect the hair. It also contains biotin, which is beneficial for hair health and growth.

Egg: helps infuse hair follicles with much-needed vitamins and minerals. Nourishing the scalp encourages new hair to grow stronger and be less prone to breakage or shedding.

Coconut Oil: is a rich source of fatty acids that can help moisturize and protect the skin's barrier function. It also has antimicrobial properties that may benefit skin health.

Honey: has natural antibacterial properties and is a humectant, which means it helps keep the skin hydrated and retains moisture. It also contains antioxidants that can help protect the skin from damage.

COMBINE:

- 1 Ripe Avocado
- 1 Egg Yolk
- 2 tablespoons of Coconut Oil
- 1 tablespoon of Honey

Instructions:

1. In a bowl, mash a ripe avocado and mix in the egg yolk, 2 tablespoons of coconut oil and 1 tablespoon of honey.
2. Apply the mixture to damp hair, distributing it evenly from root to tip.
3. Leave the mask on for 20-30 minutes. Shampoo and condition your hair as usual.
4. Repeat as needed.

Enhance the health and vitality of your hair with this nourishing Avocado Hair Mask recipe. Your locks will thank you for this rejuvenating treatment!

4.Calming Lavender and Chamomile Bath Soak

I*ngredients:*

- Epsom Salts
- Sea Salt or Himalayan Pink Salt
- Baking Soda
- Dried Lavender Flowers
- Dry Chamomile Flower
- Lavendar Essential Oil

Benefits:

Epsom Salts: it can help sooth sore muscles, relaxes the body and promotes detoxification through its rich source of magnesium. Epsom salt can also act as a gentle exfoliant, help-ing remove dead skin cells and unclog pores.

Sea Salt/Himalayan Pink Salt: rich in minerals that nour-ish the skin and enhance relaxation. The minerals also enhance the detoxifying effects of the soak.

Baking Soda: Softens the skin and helps to soothe irrita-tion.

Dry Lavender Buds: the calming scent can reduce stress, anxiety and promotes overall relaxation. It can help calm skin irritations, promote overall skin health, support muscle relaxation, alleviate headaches and aid in better sleep.

Dry Chamomile Flower: has soothing, anti-inflammatory and bacteria combating properties that can help calm the skin. Can also help to relieve skin irritation and wound healing.

Lavender Essential Oil: enhances relaxation, reduces anxiety, and creates a calming atmosphere.

Combine:

- 1 cup of Epsom Salts
- 1 cup Sea Salt or Himalayan Pink Salt
- ½ cup Baking Soda
- ¼ cup of Dried Lavender Flowers
- ¼ cup of Dried Chamomile Flowers
- 10-15 drops Lavender Essential Oil

Instructions:

1. In a large mixing bowl, combine the Epsom salt and Sea Salt or Himalayan Pink Salt. Stire well to ensure they are evenly mixed
2. Add the baking soda to the mixture and stir until fully incorporated.
3. Gently fold the dried lavender and chamomile flowers into the salt mixture. Make sure the flowers are evenly distributed throughout the mixture.
4. Add the lavender essential oil to the mix. Stir well.
5. Store in a clean dry bottle/jar/ label and date.

6. While the tub is filling, add ½ to 1 cup of the bath soak to the running water. Swirl the water gently to help dissolve the mixture.
7. Soak in the bath for at least 20-30 minutes to fully enjoy the soothing aroma and relaxation.
8. Once done, rinse your body with fresh warm water to remove any residue from the bath soak.

Make this bath soak an enjoyable addition to a self-care routine!

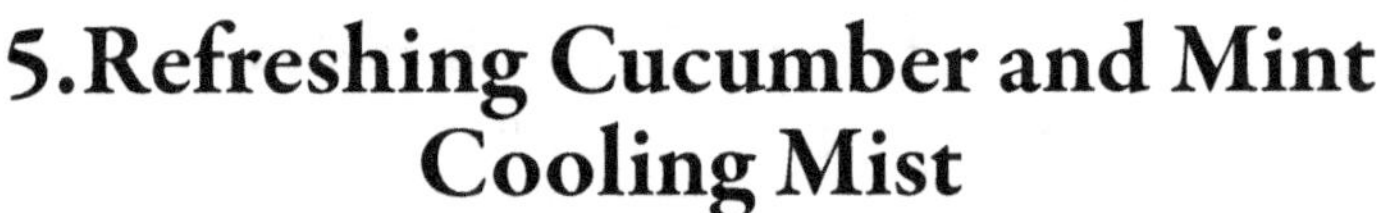

5. Refreshing Cucumber and Mint Cooling Mist

Ingredients:

- Fresh Cucumber Juice
- Mint Leaves
- Witch Hazel
- Distilled Water

Benefits:

Fresh Cucumber Juice: offers numerous benefits, including hydration due to its high-water content, skin-soothing and anti-inflammatory properties, reductions of puffiness and dark circles when applied topically and a refreshing and revitalizing effect, making it excellent addition to skincare and dietary regimes.

Mint Leaves: offer a range of benefits, including to aid digestion and soothe digestive discomfort when consumed. On skincare, mint leaves can provide a cooling and invigorating sensation, making them a useful ingredient for DIY beauty products, particularly on facial and scalp treatments.

Witch Hazel: has astringent properties that can help tone and tighten the skin. It also has anti-inflammatory and antioxidant effects and is often used to soothe skin irritation

ECO-CHIC BEAUTY: A GUIDE TO DIY SELF-CARE

Combine:

- 1 Cucumber
- Handful of Mint Leaves
- ½ cup of Witch Hazel
- Distilled water

Instructions:

1. In a blender, puree one cucumber and a handful of fresh mint leaves with ½ cup of witch hazel.
2. Strain the mixture into a spray bottle and add an equal amount of distilled water.
3. Spritz the mist onto your face as needed for a refreshing effect.
4. Store the bottle in the refrigerator and shake well before each use.

6.Soothing Aloe Vera and Green Tea Eye Gel

Ingredients:

- Aloe Vera Gel
- Chamomile Tea
- Green Tea
- Vitamin E Oil
- Lavender Essential Oil

Benefits:

Aloe Vera Gel: aloe vera gel contains polysaccharides, which have moisturizing and anti-inflammatory properties. It hydrates, soothes and calms irritated skin.

Green Tea: is rich in antioxidants and anti-inflammatory properties. It also helps reduce puffiness and dark circles.

Chamomile Tea: known for its calming effects, chamomile can help sooth irritation and redness.

Vitamin E Oil: provides moisturization, antioxidant protection, support for wound healing, scar reduction and potential anti-aging effects.

Lavender Essential Oil: Adds a calming scent and provides soothing benefits to help relax the skin.

Combine:

- 1 tablespoons of Aloe Vera Gel
- 1 tablespoon Green Tea (brewed and cooled)
- 1 tablespoon Chamomile Tea (brewed and cooled)
- 1 teaspoon Vitamin E Oil
- 1-2 drops Lavender Essential Oil

Instructions:

1. Start by brewing a strong cup of green tea and chamomile tea. 1 tea bag in ¼ cup of boiling water. Let it steep for 5-10 minutes.
2. In a bowl, combine the cooled teas.
3. Add Aloe Vera to the mixture. Stir well.
4. Add vitamin E oil. Mix well. Add lavender essential oil if adding
5. Cleans face and eye area
6. Massage the gel into the skin using a gentling tapping motion. This can help improve circulation.
7. Allow the gel to absorb into the skin. You can leave it overnight for the best results.
8. For optimal results, use this eye gel daily or as needed to help reduce puffiness and dark circles.
9. Put the eye gel in a clean jar/container and label. Store in the refrigerator for a refreshing and cooling effect.

7.Revitalizing Rose and Coconut Bath Bombs

Ingredients:

- Baking Soda
- Citric Acid
- Coconut Oil
- Rose Essential Oil
- Dried Rose Petals

Benefits:

Baking Soda: can help with gentle exfoliation and neutralizing odors. When used on skin it can be a mild exfoliant and in haircare, to clarify the scalp and remove buildup.

Citric Acid: a natural preservative that enhances skin exfoliation and adjusts the pH from cosmetic products. It can also assist in brightening the complexion and support cell turnover, while clarifying the scalp and hair.

Coconut Oil: is a rich source of fatty acids that can help moisturize and protect the skin's barrier function. Its antimicrobial properties help protect against microbial contamination.

Rose Essential Oil: has potential to soothe skin irritations while having an anti-aging and moisturizing effect.

ECO-CHIC BEAUTY: A GUIDE TO DIY SELF-CARE

Combine:

- 1 cup Baking Soda
- ½ cup Citric Acid
- 2-3 tablespoons of Coconut Oil
- 20-25 drops of Rose Essential Oil
- Dried Rose Petals (for visual effect)

Instructions:

1. In a large bowl, mix 1 cup of baking soda and ½ cup of citric acid thoroughly.
2. Slowly add 2-3 tablespoons of melted coconut oil and 20-25 drops of rose essential oil, while stirring continuously to form a textured mixture.
3. Gently fold in a small handful of dried rose petals before packing the mixture into a silicone mold and allowing it to dry for at least 24 hours.

8.Balancing Yogurt and Turmeric Face Cleanser

*I*ngredients:

- Plain Yogurt
- Turmeric Powder
- Honey
- Tea Tree Essential Oil

Benefits:

Plain Yogurt: provides gentle exfoliation and hydration while balancing the skin's natural oils. The lactic acid in yogurt may help soothe and balance the skin.

Turmeric Powder: has numerous benefits, from its potential anti-inflammatory and antioxidant properties, to brightening one's complexion, reducing redness and soothing skin irritations.

Honey: natural antiseptic and antibacterial properties make it beneficial for promoting wound healing and reducing the risk of infection. In skincare, honey helps hydrate and alleviate minor irritations.

ECO-CHIC BEAUTY: A GUIDE TO DIY SELF-CARE

Tea Tree Essential Oil: is renowned for its antibacterial, ant-inflammatory and anti-fungal properties, making it a valuable ingredient in skincare that addresses various skin concerns such as acne and irritation.

Combine:

- 2 tablespoons of Plain Yogurt
- ½ teaspoons of Turmeric Powder
- 1 teaspoon of Honey
- 4-5 drops of Tea Tree Essential Oil

Instructions:

1. In a bowl, mix 2 tablespoons of plain yogurt, ½ teaspoon of turmeric powder, 1 teaspoon of honey, and 4-5 drops of tea tree essential oil.
2. Apply the cleanser to damp skin, massage gently, rinse with warm water.
3. This balancing cleanser is safe to use daily.

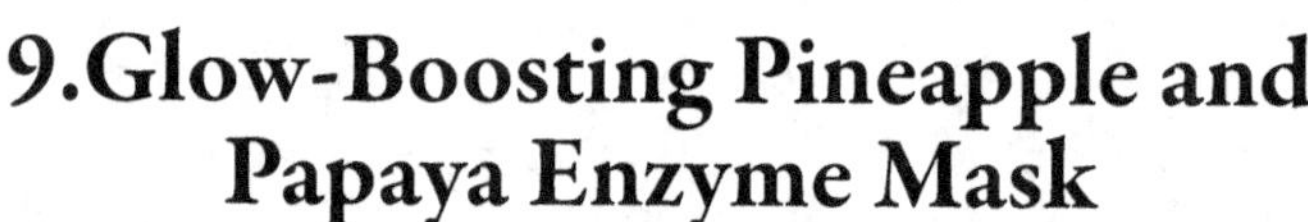

9.Glow-Boosting Pineapple and Papaya Enzyme Mask

Ingredients:

- Fresh Pineapple
- Ripe Papaya
- Raw Honey
- Lemon Juice

Benefits:

Pineapple: contains natural enzymes, such as bromelain which can provide gentle exfoliation and promote skin renewal. These enzymes may also help remove dead skin cells.

Papaya: containing papain, can help remove dead skin cells, brighten the complexion and promote a smoother skin texture.

Raw Honey: a natural antibacterial with natural humectant, that helps hydrate and soothe the skin. It can also assist with gentle exfoliation and may contribute to a clearer and more radiant complexion.

Lemon Juice: The natural citric acid may act as a mild exfoliant and help brighten the skin. It may also contribute to oil control and skin brightening. Individuals with sensitive and dry skin are urged to use caution when using lemon juice on skin as it can cause irritation or dryness.

Combine:

- ¼ - ½ cup Fresh Pineapple
- ¼ - ½ cup Ripe Papaya
- 1 tablespoon of Raw Honey
- 1 teaspoon of Lemon Juice

Instructions:

1. In a blender, puree equal parts of fresh pineapple and ripe papaya.
2. Transfer the fruit puree to a bowl and add 1 tablespoon of raw honey and 1 teaspoon of lemon juice. Mix well.
3. Apply the mask to clean, dry skin and leave it on for 15-20 minutes before rinsing with warm water.

10. Herbal Hair Rinse for Shine and Scalp Health

Ingredients:

- Apple Cider Vinegar
- Dried Rosemary
- Dried Lavender
- Filtered Water

Benefits:

Apple Cider Vinegar: can help balance the scalp's pH, remove product buildup, and impart creating a smooth appearance. It can also seal the hair cuticle, reduce frizz and promote overall health.

Dried Rosemary: contributes to scalp health and hair vitality due to its antibacterial properties and potential to stimulate hair follicles. It may also address dandruff, create a healthier scalp environment, and contribute to a refreshing and invigorating hair care experience.

Dried Lavender: offers a calming and aromatic hair care experience. May also contribute to scalp health and relaxation.

Combine:

- 2-3 tablespoons of Apple Cider Vinegar

ECO-CHIC BEAUTY: A GUIDE TO DIY SELF-CARE

- 2 tablespoons of Dried Rosemary
- 2 tablespoons of Dried Lavender
- 4 cups of Filtered Water

Instructions:

1. In a large bowl, combine 2-3 tablespoons of apple cider vinegar with 2 tablespoons each of dried rosemary and dried lavender.
2. Pour 4 cups of filtered water over the ingredients and let the mixture steep for 30-60 minutes.
3. It is important to strain the rosemary and lavender infusion before use to avoid any debris in the hair.
4. After shampooing, pour the herbal rinse over your hair and massage it into your scalp. Leave it in for a few minutes before rinsing with cool water.
5. It is advised to incorporate a vinegar hair rinse into your routine once or twice a week and observe how your scalp and hair respond. If trying for the first time, try a patch test first to ensure it's well tolerated.

11.Soothing Coconut and Shea Butter Body Lotion

Ingredients:

- Shea Butter
- Coconut Oil
- Almond Oil
- Essential Oil(s) of choice

Benefits:

Shea Butter: is deeply moisturizing and nourishing, as well as soothing and hydrating for dry skin.

Coconut Oil: offers deep hydration, skin softening, and provides a protective barrier; providing a smoother and more supple complexion.

Almond Oil: has a deep hydrating and emollient properties, it soothes and softens the skin while rich in vitamins and antioxidants. Its light texture provides a quick absorption, making it a popular choice for those with dry and sensitive skin.

Essential Oils: aromatherapeutic properties include reduced stress and improved mood. On skin, these oils moisturize, sooth and tone. Antimicrobial properties help protect against microbial contamination.

Combine:

- ½ cup Shea Butter
- ¼ cup Coconut Oil
- 4 tablespoons Almond Oil
- Optional: a few drops of your preferred essential oil for fragrance (such as lavender or vanilla)

Instructions:

1. In a heat-safe bowl, combine the shea butter, coconut oil and almond oil.
2. Create a double boiler by placing the bowl over a pot of simmering water, ensuring the water doesn't touch the bottom of the bowl.
3. Gently melt the shea butter, coconut oil and almond oil together, stirring occasionally until completely melted.
4. Remove the bowl from the heat and allow the mixture to cool for a few minutes.
5. If using, add a few drops of your preferred essential oil for fragrance and mix well.
6. Transfer the mixture to a clean, airtight container or jar for storage.

12.Eucalyptus and Peppermint Foot Soak

Ingredients:

- Epsom Salt
- Sea Salt
- Baking Soda
- Eucalyptus Essential Oil
- Peppermint Essential Oil

Benefits:

Epsom Salt: can also act as a gentle exfoliant, helping remove dead skin cells and unclog pores. Also, a rich source of magnesium.

Sea Salt: is a natural exfoliant that helps remove dead skin cells, unclogs pores, and can help with conditions such as acne or eczema. It also contains minerals that are beneficial for the skin, such as magnesium and calcium.

Baking Soda: A gentle exfoliant that can help in removing dead skin cells. Baking soda also has natural deodorizing and cleansing properties.

Eucalyptus Essential Oil: Its natural antibacterial and antifungal properties help purify and clean the feet.

ECO-CHIC BEAUTY: A GUIDE TO DIY SELF-CARE

Peppermint Essential Oil: is known for its cooling, soothing and relaxing effect.

Combine:

- ½ cup Epsom Salt
- ¼ cup Sea Salt
- ¼ cup Baking Soda
- 5-7 drops of Eucalyptus Essential Oil
- 5-7 drops of Peppermint Essential Oil

Instructions:

1. In a large bowl, combine the Epsom salt, sea salt, and baking soda.
2. Add the eucalyptus and peppermint essential oils to the salt mixture.
3. Stir the ingredients thoroughly to distribute the oils evenly.
4. Add ¼ to ½ cup of the foot soak mixture to a basin or foot spa filled with warm water.
5. Soak your feet for 15-20 minutes, then pat your feet dry.
6. Store the foot soak in a clean, airtight container or use it immediately.

13. Acne-Fighting Tea Tree and Witch Hazel Toner

Ingredients:

- Witch Hazel
- Aloe Vera Gel
- Tea Tree Essential Oil
- Filtered Water

Benefits:

Witch Hazel: has astringent properties that can help tone and tighten the skin. It also has anti-inflammatory and antioxidant effects and is often used to soothe skin irritation.

Aloe Vera Gel: has soothing and moisturizing properties and contains compounds that can help reduce inflammation and support wound healing. It's often used to calm irritated or sunburned skin.

Tea Tree Essential Oil: its natural antibacterial properties and anti-inflammatory properties can help in combating various skin issues such as acne and inflammation. Tea tree oil can also assist in clarifying *and balancing the skin,*
making it great for those with oily or acne prone skin.
Combine:

ECO-CHIC BEAUTY: A GUIDE TO DIY SELF-CARE

- ½ cup Witch Hazel
- ¼ cup pure Aloe Vera Gel
- 10 drops Tea Tree Essential Oil
- Optional: 1-2 drops of Lavender Essential Oil

Instructions:

1. In a clean, sterile bottle, combine the witch hazel and pure aloe vera gel.
2. Add the tea tree essential oil (and optional lavender oil if desired) to the mixture for skin soothing properties.
3. Close the bottle and shake well to ensure the ingredients are thoroughly mixed.
4. To use, apply the toner to a cotton pad and sweep it over the skin after cleansing.
5. Store the toner in a cool, dark place and allow it to sit for several hours or overnight before use.

This toner can help to remove traces of makeup or dirt, reduce excess oil, and soothe acne-prone skin thanks to the astringent and antibacterial properties of witch hazel and tea tree oil

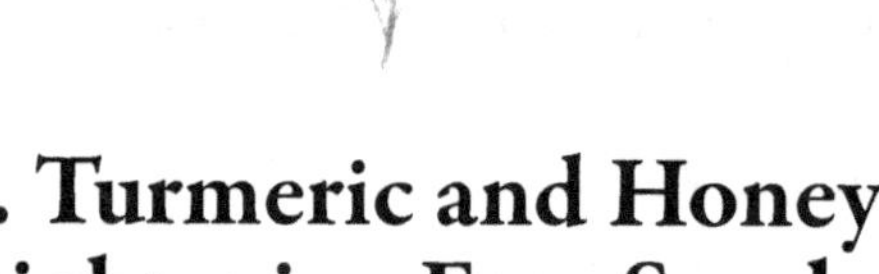

14. Turmeric and Honey Brightening Face Scrub

Ingredients:

- Turmeric
- Raw Honey
- Plain Yogurt
- Oats (finely ground)

Benefits:

Turmeric: has numerous benefits when used in skincare, from its potential anti-inflammatory and antioxidant properties, to brightening one's complexion, reducing redness and soothing skin irritations.

Raw Honey: natural antiseptic and antibacterial properties make it beneficial for promoting wound healing and reducing the risk of infection. In skincare, honey helps hydrate and alleviate minor irritations.

Plain Yogurt: provides gentle exfoliation and hydration while balancing the skin's natural oils. The lactic acid in yogurt may help soothe and balance the skin, addressing certain skin concerns.

ECO-CHIC BEAUTY: A GUIDE TO DIY SELF-CARE

Oats: a gentle exfoliant that contains anti-inflammatory properties. They can also have a soothing effect making them suitable for sensitive/easily irritated skin.

Combine:

- 1 tablespoon Turmeric
- 2 tablespoons Raw Honey (preferably raw honey)
- 2 tablespoons Plain Yogurt
- 1-2 tablespoons Oats (finely ground)

Instructions:

1. In a small bowl, combine the turmeric powder, honey and plain yogurt.
2. Gradually add the oats to the mixture and stir until you reach a desired scrub consistency.
3. To use, apply the mixture to clean, damp skin, and gently massage in a circular motion.
4. Rinse thoroughly with warm water and pat skin dry.

15. Calendula and Rose Infused Facial Steam

*I*ngredients:

- Dried Calendula Flowers
- Dried Rose Petals
- Large bowl of Hot Water

Benefits:

Dried Calendula Flowers: is known for its soothing and skin- nourishing properties. When used in a facial steam, it can help to promote a calming and revitalizing experience, while providing anti-inflammatory effects, making it a suitable choice for those with sensitive or irritated skin.

Dried Rose Petals: the natural oils present in rose petals can help to hydrate and nourish the skin. The aromatic, calming and soothing aroma contributes to a relaxing and rejuvenating experience, making them luxurious addition to facial steam

Combine:

- ¼ cup Dried Calendula Flowers
- ¼ cup Dried Rose Petals
- 4 cups Boiling Water
- Optional: A few drops of essential oil of choice, such

as lavender or chamomile

Instructions:

1. Place the dried calendula flowers and rose petals in a large heat-safe bowl.
2. Carefully pour the boiling water over the dried flowers.
3. If using, add a few drops of the preferred essential oil.
4. Lean over the bowl, drape a towel over your head to create a tent, and steam your face for 10-15 minutes.
5. Be cautious of the steam's temperature and do not place your face too close to the hot water to avoid scalding.

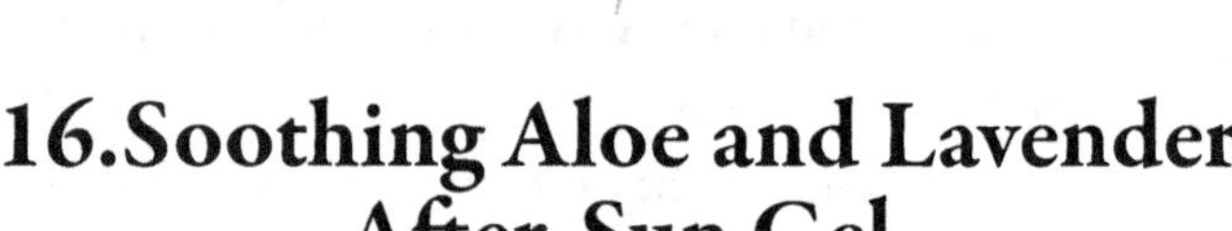

16.Soothing Aloe and Lavender After-Sun Gel

*I*ngredients:

- Aloe Vera Gel
- Lavender Essential Oil
- Vitamin E Oil

Benefits:

Aloe Vera Gel: has a hydrating, soothing and cooling effect making it great for sensitive skin types. It is also great for wound healing, inflammation, cuts and burns.

Lavender Essential Oil: known for its soothing and calming properties, which can help alleviate discomfort and promote skin recovery after sun exposure. The cooling and anti-inflammatory properties of lavender oil may help to reduce skin irritation, making it a valuable addition to an after-sun skincare product.

Vitamin E Oil: offers a range of potential benefits, including moisturization, antioxidant protection, support for wound healing, scar reduction and potential anti-aging effects. It provides nourishment and protects the skin.

Combine:

ECO-CHIC BEAUTY: A GUIDE TO DIY SELF-CARE

- ½ cup pure Aloe Vera Gel
- 10-15 drops of Lavender Essential Oil
- ¼ cup Vitamin E Oil
- Optional: 1-2 tablespoons of Coconut Oil

Instructions:

1. In a clean bowl, combine the pure aloe vera gel with, lavender essential oil, vitamin E oil and coconut oil (if using).
2. Stir the mixture thoroughly to ensure the essential oil is evenly distributed.
3. Apply the after-sun gel generously to the skin.
4. Transfer the gel to a clean, airtight container for storage.
5. It's important to store the gel in a cool place and discontinue use if you experience any skin sensitivity.

17. Rosemary and Mint Scalp Scrub

Ingredients:

- Fine Sea Salt
- Coconut Oil
- Fresh Rosemary
- Fresh Mint
- Peppermint Essential Oil

Benefits:

Sea Salt: is a natural exfoliant that helps remove dead skin cells, unclogs pores, and can help with conditions such as acne or eczema. It also contains minerals that are beneficial for the skin, such as magnesium and calcium.

Coconut Oil: is a rich source of fatty acids that can help moisturize and protect the skin's barrier function. It also has antimicrobial properties that may benefit skin health.

Fresh Rosemary: contributes to scalp health and hair vitality due to its antibacterial properties and potential to stimulate hair follicles. It may also address dandruff, create a healthier scalp environment, and contribute to a refreshing and invigorating hair care experience.

Fresh Mint: has antimicrobial properties which can help with dandruff and scalp issues, while enhancing circulation.

ECO-CHIC BEAUTY: A GUIDE TO DIY SELF-CARE

Combine:

- ½ cup Sea Salt
- ¼ cup Coconut Oil
- 2 tablespoons Fresh Rosemary, finely chopped
- 2 tablespoons Fresh Mint, finely chopped
- 10-15 drops Peppermint Essential Oil

Instructions:

1. In a bowl, combine the sea salt and carrier oil. Mix well.
2. Add the finely chopped fresh rosemary and mint to the salt and oil mix.
3. Add the peppermint essential oil and stir thoroughly to distribute the oil evenly.
4. Apply a small amount of the scrub to a damp scalp and massage gently for several minutes.
5. Rinse thoroughly and shampoo as usual.
6. Transfer the scrub to a clean airtight container for storage.

18. Rejuvenating Green Tea and Honey Face Mask

I*ngredients:*

- Green Tea Leaves
- Honey
- Plain Yogurt (Optional)

Benefits:

Green Tea Leaves: are rich in antioxidants, particularly catechins, which can help protect the skin from environmental damage. It also has anti-inflammatory properties and may help promote skin health.

Honey: has natural antibacterial properties and is a humectant, which means it helps keep the skin hydrated and retains moisture. It also contains antioxidants that can help protect the skin from damage.

Plain Yogurt: is a gentle exfoliant, promoting a smoother and brighter complex. It also locks in moister while hydrating the skin. Natural fats and proteins can help balance natural oils. May also combat acne causing bacteria.

Combine:

- 1 tablespoon Green Tea Leaves (or contents of 1

green tea bag)
- 1 tablespoon Honey (preferably raw honey)
- 1-2 tablespoons of Pain Yogurt for additional soothing properties (optional)

Instructions:

1. Steep the green tea leaves in 1-2 tablespoons of hot water and allow it to cool.
2. In a small bowl, combine the brewed green tea leaves with the honey.
3. If using, add the plain yogurt to the mixture and mix well.
4. Apply the mask to a clean, dry face and leave it on for 10-15 minutes.
5. Rinse off with warm water and pat the skin dry.

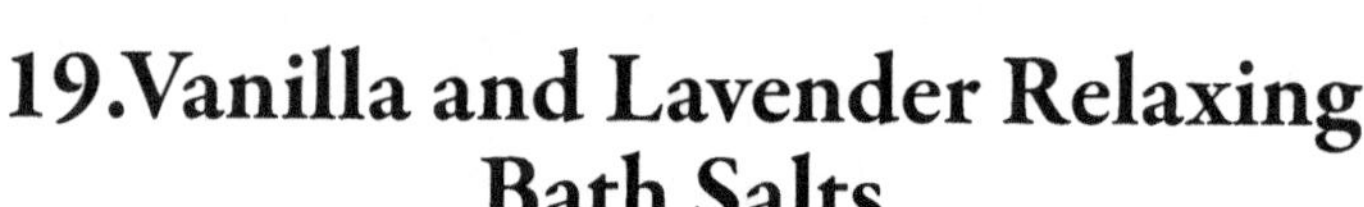

19.Vanilla and Lavender Relaxing Bath Salts

Ingredients:

- Epsom Salt
- Sea Salt
- Baking Soda
- Vanilla Essential Oil
- Lavender Essential Oil
- Dried Lavender Buds (optional for visual)

Benefits:

Epsom Salt: can also act as a gentle exfoliant, helping remove dead skin cells and unclog pores. Also, a rich source of magnesium.

Sea Salt: is a natural exfoliant that helps remove dead skin cells, unclogs pores, and can help with conditions such as acne or eczema. It also contains minerals that are beneficial for the skin, such as magnesium and calcium.

Baking Soda: a gentle exfoliant that can help in removing dead skin cells. Baking soda also has natural deodorizing and cleansing properties.

ECO-CHIC BEAUTY: A GUIDE TO DIY SELF-CARE

Vanilla Essential Oil: using vanilla essential oil in a bath soak provides a calming and comforting aroma that promotes relaxation, tranquility and may help reduce stress and anxiety. Its antioxidant properties help nourish the skin, while the sweet scent can uplift your mood and create a sense of emotional well-being. Additionally, vanilla essential oil's soothing qualities can alleviate skin irritation, making your bath experience not only fragrance but also beneficial for your skin.

Lavender Essential Oil: renowned for its calming and relaxing properties, it makes this oil an excellent choice for reducing stress and anxiety. Its soothing aroma can promote better sleep and enhance overall mood, creating a tranquil atmosphere. Additionally, it has anti-inflammatory and antiseptic properties which can help soothe irritated skin and promote healing.

Combine:

- 1 cup Epsom Salt
- ½ cup Sea Salt
- ¼ cup Baking Soda
- 10-15 drops of Vanilla Essential Oil
- 10-15 drops Lavender Essential Oil
- Dried Lavender Buds (optional for visual appeal)

Instructions:

1. In a large bowl, thoroughly mix the Epsom salt, sea salt and baking soda.
2. Add the drops of vanilla and lavender essential oils to the salt mixture and stir to distribute the oils evenly.
3. If desired, mix the dried lavender buds for added

fragrance and visual appeal.

4. Add a couple of tablespoons to the bath experience.
5. Store in a airtight container, away from moisture and direct sunlight.

20. Coconut and Coffee under eye dark circle treatment

Ingredients:

- Almond Oil
- Coconut Oil
- Ground Coffee
- Honey
- Aloe Vera Gel

Benefits:

Almond Oil: rich in vitamin E, it nourishes and hydrates the delicate under-eye skin., helping to reduce dark circles and fine lines.

Coconut Oil: provides deep moisture and has anti-inflammatory properties that soothe the skin.

Ground Coffee: the caffeine helps to constrict blood vessels, reducing the appearance of dark circles and puffiness.

Honey: a natural humectant that hydrates the skin, honey also has anti-inflammatory properties for sensitive skin.

Aloe Vera Gel: soothes and hydrates the skin, reducing inflammation and discomfort, and promoting healing.

Combine:

- 1 tablespoon Almond Oil
- 1 tablespoon Coconut Oil
- 1 teaspoon Ground Coffee
- 1 teaspoon Honey
- 1 teaspoon Aloe Vera Gel

Instructions:

1. Combine the almond oil and coconut oil. Stir well until thoroughly mixed.
2. Add coffee grounds (fresh or left over), honey and aloe vera gel to the oil mixture. Mix well.
3. Optional: 1 drop of lavender essential oil.
4. Store in a clean jar/container and label.
5. Start with a clean, dry face.
6. Apply a small amount gently under your eyes.
7. Massage in the eye area for a few minutes using a circular motion.
8. Leave on for 15-20 minutes or overnight.
9. Rinse with lukewarm water.
10. Finish with your regular moisturizer.

21. Castor oil and Aloe Vera Hair Thickening Mask

Ingredients:

- Castor Oil
- Aloe Vera Gel
- Coconut Oil
- Rosemary Essential Oil
- Peppermint Essential Oil

Benefits:

Castor Oil: Know for promoting hair growth and strengthening the hair shaft.

Aloe Vera Gel: has a hydrating, soothing and cooling effect making it great for sensitive skin types. It is also great for wound healing, inflammation, cuts and burns.

Coconut Oil: is a rich source of fatty acids that can help moisturize and protect the skin's barrier function. It also has antimicrobial properties that may benefit skin health.

Rosemary Essential oil: known for stimulating hair growth and improving scalp health.

Peppermint Essential Oil: helps to invigorate the scalp and encourage hair growth.

Combine:

- 2 tablespoons of Castor Oil
- 2 tablespoons of Aloe Vera
- 1 tablespoon coconut oil
- 5-10 drops of Rosemary Essential Oil
- 5-10 drops of Peppermint Essential Oil

Instructions:

1. In a small bowl, combine the castor oil, aloe vera gentle, and coconut oil. Stir until well blended.
2. Add the rosemary and peppermint oil to the mixture and stir again to combine.
3. Slightly warm the mixture in a double boiler or microwave (just a few seconds); ensure it's not too hot to put on scalp.
4. Part your hair into sections and apply the mixture directly on scalp, massage gently with your fingertips. Work any remining mixture through the length of your hair.
5. Cover your hair with a shower cap or warm towel and leave the mask on for at least 30 mins. For deeper conditioning, you can leave it overnight.
6. Rinse your hair with a gentle shampoo to remove the oil. You might need to shampoo twice to ensure the residue is gone.
7. Follow up with your usual condition if needed.
8. Use this once a week for best results

22. Nail Strengthening Oil

Ingredients:

- Jojoba Oil
- Vitamin E Oil
- 1 tablespoon Almond Oil
- 5 drops Lavendar Essential Oil
- 5 drips Lemon Essential Oil

Benefits:

Jojoba Oil: Is rich in vitamins and minerals that nourish and strengthen nails. Jojoba Oil also mimics the natural oils of our skin, providing deep hydration and promoting strong, flexible nails.

Vitamin E Oil: offers a range of potential benefits, including moisturization, antioxidant protection, support for wound healing, scar reduction and potential anti-aging effects. An antioxidant that helps to repair and protect the nails from damage, promoting healthy growth.

Almond Oil: rich in vitamin E, A and B, it deeply nourishes and strengthens nails, preventing breakage and promoting growth. has a deep hydrating and emollient properties, it soothes and softens the skin.

Lavendar Essential Oil: known for its calming properties, it also promotes nail growth and can help to heal any minor cuts or infections around the nail bed.

Lemon Essential Oil: brightens and strengthens nails while providing antifungal benefits, helping your nails to be healthy and strong.

Combine:

- 2 tablespoons Jojoba Oil
- 1 tablespoon Vitamin E Oil
- 1 tablespoon Almond Oil
- 5 drops Lavender Essential Oil
- 5 drops Lemon Essential Oil

Instructions:

1. In a small bowl, combine the jojoba oil, vitamin E oil, and almond oi. Stir well to ensure they are thoroughly mixed.
2. Add the lavender essential oil and lemon essential oil. Stir to combine all the ingredients.
3. Using a small funnel or dropper, carefully transfer the mixture into a clean sterilized bottle.
4. Before putting the mixture on, ensure that your hands are washed and dried. Ensure that nail polish is removed.
5. Using a brush of a nail polish bottle or a dropper, apply the small amount of the oil to each nail and cuticle.
6. *Massage gently for a few minutes in a circular motion.*

This helps stimulate blood flow and encourages absorption of nutrients.

7. *Allow the oil to absorb fully. It's best to do this treatment before bed to let the oils work overnight.*

Additional tips for stronger Nails:

- Diet: Ensure you are consuming a balanced diet rich in vitamins and minerals, particularly biotin, which is known to promote nail health.

- Hydration: Keep your body and nails hydrated by drinking plenty of water and moisturizing your hands and nails regularly.

- Gentle care: avoid using your nails as tools to open or scrap things. Keep them trimmed and filed to prevent breakage.

- Protection: wear gloves when doing household chores, especially when using cleaning products or exposing your hands to water for extended periods.

23.Clarifying Shampoo

I*ngredients:*

- Liquid Castile Soap
- Distilled Water
- Apple Cider Vinegar
- Baking Soda
- Aloe Vera
- Tea Tree Essential Oil
- Lemon Essential Oil
- Peppermint Essential Oil

Benefits:

Liquid Castile Soap: a biodegradable, gentle cleanser that effectively removes dirt and buildup without harsh chemicals.

Distilled water: dilute the shampoo and help distribute the ingredients evenly.

Apple Cider Vinegar: removes product buildup and excess oil from the scalp and hair, leading to a cleaner, healthier appearance. Its natural acidity helps balance the scalp's pH, promoting shine and smoothness while preventing frizz. Additionally, ACV has antimicrobial properties that can help maintain scalp health and reduce dandruff. It revitalizes hair, leaving it fresh and vibrant.

Baking Soda: can help with gentle exfoliation and neutralizing odors. When used on skin it can be a mild exfoliant and in haircare, to clarify the scalp, remove buildup and stubborn residue.

Aloe Vera Gel: helps soothe, hydrate and moisturize the scalp, counteracting the potential drying effects of the clarifying agents.

Tea Tree Essential Oil: provides antifungal and antibacterial properties, promoting a healthy scalp. Tea tree oil can also assist in clarifying and balancing the skin.

Lemon Essential Oil: helps remove excess oil and buildup from the scalp and hair, leaving it feeling clean and refreshed. It also has natural antimicrobial properties that help to cleanse the scalp, reduce dandruff and promote a healthy environment. Lemon essential oil is also a shine enhancer, making it look vibrant and healthy. Naturally clarifies the hair and adds a refreshing scent.

Peppermint Essential Oil: stimulates the scalp, promoting circulation and hair growth, while adding a cooling sensation.

Combine:

- ¼ cup liquid Castile Soap
- ¼ cup Distilled Water
- 1 tablespoon Apple Cider Vinegar
- 1 teaspoon Baking Soda
- 1 tablespoon Aloe Vera Gel
- 10 drops Tea Tree Essential Oil
- 10 drops Lemon Essential Oil
- 5 drops Peppermint Essential Oil

Instructions:

1. Gather all your ingredients and ensure your workspace is clean. Have a clean, empty bottle ready for your shampoo.
2. Combine the liquid castile soap and distilled water in a bowl; stir gently to avoid too many bubbles.
3. Add the apple cider vinegar and baking soda. Stir well to ensure they are fully incorporated. The mixture might fix a little due to the reaction between the vinegar and baking soda, this is normal.
4. Add the aloe vera gel to the mixture.
5. Add the tee tree essential oil, lemon essential oil and peppermint essential oil.
6. Stir and ensure all ingredients are mixed properly.
7. Using a funnel, carefully pour the shampoo into a clean container.
8. Use as you would your regular shampoo. Rinse with warm water.
9. Use once a week, or as needed.

24. Coconut and Aloe Vera Hair Conditioner

Ingredients:

- Coconut Oil
- Shea Butter
- Aloe Vera Gel
- Apple Cider Vinegar
- Lavendar Essential Oil
- Rosemary Essential Oil
- Peppermint Essential Oil
- Jojoba Oil

Benefits:

Coconut Oil: deeply moisturizes the hair, adds shine, and helps to reduce protein loss.

Shea Butter: rich in Vitamins A and E, it nourishes and softens the hair, providing deep hydration.

Aloe Vera Gel: hydrates the hair and scalp, promotes healthy hair growth, and sooths irritations.

Apple Cider Vinegar: balances the scalp's pH, adds shine, and helps to detangle hair.

Lavendar Essential Oil: sooths the scalp, reduces dandruff, and provides a calming scent.

Rosemary Essential Oil: stimulates hair growth, improves scalp health, and helps to prevent hair loss.

Peppermint Essential Oil: invigorates the scalp, promotes circulation, and provides a refreshing sensation.

Jojoba Oil: mimics the scalp's natural oils, provding deep hydration without leaving a greasy residue.

Combine:

- ½ cup Coconut Oil
- ¼ cup Shea Butter
- ¼ cup Aloe Vera
- 1 tablespoon Apple Cider Vinegar
- 10 drops Lavender Essential Oil
- 10 drops Rosemary Essential Oil
- 5 drops peppermint Essential oil
- 1 tablespoon Jojoba Oil

Instructions:

1. In a double boiler or a heat safe bowl over a pot of simmering water, combine the coconut oil and shea butter. Stir occasionally until ingredients are combined.
2. Remove the mixture from heat and let it cool slightly. You want it to be warm but not hot.
3. Add Aloe Vera Gel and Apple Cider Vinegar to the mixture. Stir thoroughly.
4. Add Lavendar, Rosemary, peppermint essential oil and jojoba oil. Stir well.
5. Using a hand mixer or a whisk, whip the mixture for

a few minutes until it becomes light, fluffy and creamy.

6. Transfer into a clean, dry container
7. Shampoo your hair as per usual
8. Apply the conditioner to hair, focusing on the mid-length to ends.
9. Massage the conditioner in your hair and let it sit for 5-10 minutes.
10. Rinse thoroughly with lukewarm water until the conditioner is washed out.

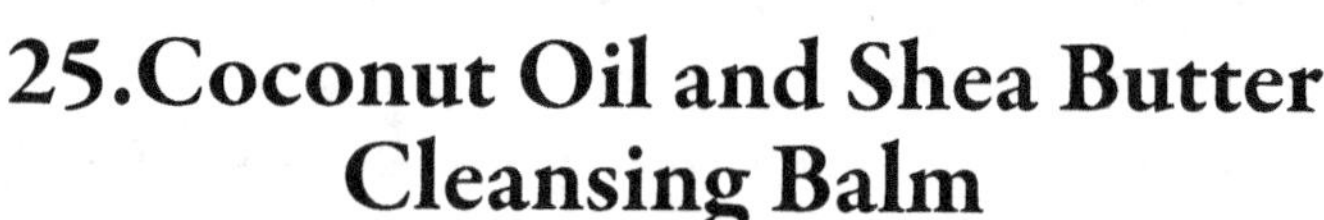

25. Coconut Oil and Shea Butter Cleansing Balm

Ingredients:

- Coconut Oil
- Shea Butter
- Almond Oil
- Beeswax Pellets
- Lavender Essential Oil
- Chamomile Essential Oil
- Tea Tree Oil

Benefits:

Coconut Oil: a natural emollient that deeply moisturizes the skin and effectively removes makeup and impurities.

Shea Butter: rich in vitamins A and E, it nourishes and hydrates the skin, providing a creamy texture to the balm.

Almond Oil: a lightweight oil that helps to dissolve make up without clogging pores, adding extra moisture to the skin.

Beeswax: provides a protective barrier on the skin, helping to lock in moisture and giving the balm its solid consistency.

Lavender Essential Oil: sooths and calms the skin, reducing redness and irritation.

Chamomile Essential Oil: known for its anti-inflammatory properties, it is ideal for sensitive skin and helps to soothe and calm the skin.

Tea Tree Oil: offers antibacterial and antimicrobial benefits, helping to keep the skin clear and healthy.

Combine:

- ¼ cup Coconut Oil
- ¼ cup Shea Butter
- ¼ cup Almond Oil
- 2 tablespoons Beeswax Pellets
- 10 drops Lavender Essential Oil
- 10 drops Chamomile Essential Oil
- 5 drops Tea Tree Oil

INSTRUCTIONS:

1. Melt the coconut oil, shea butter, almond oil and beeswax pallets in a double boiler or heat safe bowl over a pot of simmering water. Stir occasionally.
2. Remove from heat once well combined. Let the mixture cool slightly to be warm.
3. Add all the essential oils to the mixture. Stir thoroughly to ensure the essential oils are evenly distributed.
4. Allow the balm to cool and solidify completely. Store the balm in a clean jar.
5. Scoop a small amount with clean dry hands. Warm between your fingers to melt the oils.

6. Massage the balm onto dry skin, focusing on the areas with make up or impurities.
7. Rinse off with warm water or using a damp cloth.

Tip: If your balm is too soft, store it in a cooler place. If it's too hard, let it sit at room temperature.

26. Anti-Aging Face Cream

Ingredients:

- Shea Butter
- Coconut Oil
- Jojoba Oil
- Rosehip Seed Oil
- Argan Oil
- Beeswax Pallets
- Frankincense Essential Oil
- Lavender Essential Oil
- Carrot Seed Essential Oil
- Vitamin E Oil

Benefits:

Shea Butter: deeply Moisturizes, promotes skin elasticity, and reduces inflammation.

Coconut Oil: hydrates the skin and provides antioxidant protection against free radicals

Jojoba Oil: balances the skin's natural oils, providing deep hydration without clogging pores.

Rosehip Seed Oil: rich in essential fatty acids and antioxidants, it helps to reduce the appearance of fine lines and improve skin tone and texture.

Argan Oil: nourishes and protects the skin with its high content of vitamin E and fatty acids.

Beeswax: helps to thicken the cream and create a protective barrier on the skin, locking in moisture.

Frankincense Essential Oil: known for its anti-aging properties, it helps to reduce the appearance of wrinkles and fine lines.

Lavender Essential Oil: sooths the skin and promotes a youthful glow.

Carrot Seed Essential Oil: rejuvenates the skin and reduces signs of aging with its powerful antioxidants.

Vitamin E Oil: Acts as a natural preservative and provides additional antioxidant benefits to protect the skin from damage.

Combine:

- ¼ cup Shea Butter
- ¼ cup Coconut Oil
- 2 tablespoons Jojoba Oil
- 1 tablespoon Rosehip Seed Oil
- 1 tablespoon Argan Oil
- 1 tablespoon Beeswax Pellets
- 10 drops Frankincense Essential Oil
- 10 drops Lavender Essential Oil
- 5 drops Carrot Seed Essential Oil
- 5 drops Vitamin E Oil

Instructions:

1. Combine the Shea butter, coconut oil, jojoba oil, rosehip seed oil, argan oil and beeswax pellets in a

double broiler or heat save bowl over a pot of simmering water. Stir until all ingredients are melted and well combined.

2. Remove from heat to let it solidify. Ensure the mixture is still warm for next step
3. Add the essentials oils, along with Vitamin E Oil.
4. Whip the mixture for a few minutes with a hand mixture or whisk. Store in a clean jar/container.
5. *Cleanse face*
6. *Apply a small amount of the cream, focusing on areas prone to fine lines and wrinkles, such as around the eyes, mouth and forehead.*
7. *Use daily. For best results, use the face cream daily, preferably at night, to allow the ingredients to work while you sleep.*

27.Soothing Face Cream for Rosacea

*I*ngredients:

- Colloidal Oatmeal
- Aloe Vera Gel
- Manuka Honey
- Rose water
- Chamomile Tea
- Lavender Essential Oil

Benefits:

Colloidal Oatmeal: provides anti-inflammatory and soothing benefits, reducing redness and irritation.

Aloe Vera Gel: hydrates and soothes the skin, reducing inflammation and promoting healing.

Manuka Honey: offers antibacterial and anti-inflammatory properties, promoting healing and calming the skin.

Rose water: soothes and tones the skin, reducing redness and providing a calming effect.

Chamomile Tea: known for its calming and anti-inflammatory properties, it helps to soothe sensitive skin.

Lavender Essential Oil: Calms the skin, reduces redness, and provides a pleasant scent.

Combine:

ECO-CHIC BEAUTY: A GUIDE TO DIY SELF-CARE

- 2 tablespoons Colloidal Oatmeal
- 1 tablespoon Aloe Vera Gel
- 1 tablespoon Manuka Honey
- 1 tablespoon Rose Water
- 1 tablespoon Chamomile Tea
- 2-3 drops Lavender Essential Oil (optional)

Instructions:

1. Brew 1 chamomile tea bag in ¼ cup of boiling water. Allow it to steep for 10 minutes then remove the tea bag and let the tea cool.
2. In a small bowl, combine the colloidal oatmeal, aloe vera gel and manuka honey. stir well.
3. Add the rose water and cooled chamomile tea to the mixture. Stir well.
4. Add the lavender essential oil if using.
5. Start with a cleansed face. Apply the mask evenly on your face, avoiding the eye area.
6. Allow the mask to sit for 15-20 minutes.
7. Rinse gently with lukewarm water.
8. Pat dry and moisturize with a gentle moisturizer.

A few Tips on managing rosacea:

- *Cold compresses help reduce redness and inflammation.*
- *Use gentle cleansers and moisturize regularly*
- *Sunscreen is essential*
- *Avoid heavy make up*
- *Incorporate anti-inflammatory foods*
- *Stay hydrated*

28. Clarifying and Nourishing Makeup Remover

Ingredients:

- Jojoba Oil
- Almond Oil
- Castor Oil
- Aloe Vera Gel
- Witch Hazel
- Tea Tree Essential Oil
- Lavender Essential Oil
- Vitamin E Oil

Benefits:

Jojoba Oil: mimic the skin's natural oils, providing dep hydration and effectively dissolving makeup and impurities.

Almond Oil: lightweight and non-comedogenic, it helps to remove make up while moisturizing and nourishing the skin.

Castor Oil: known for its deep cleansing properties, it helps to clarify the skin and remove stubborn make up.

Aloe Vera Gel: soothes and hydrates the skin, providing a calming effect and reducing inflammation.

Witch Hazel: a natural astringent that helps to clarify the skin, tighten pores, and reduce inflammation.

ECO-CHIC BEAUTY: A GUIDE TO DIY SELF-CARE

Tea Tree Essential Oil: provides antibacterial and anti-inflammatory benefits, helping to keep the skin clear and healthy.

Lavender Essential Oil: soothes the skin and provides a calming scent, promoting relaxation.

Vitamin E Oil: acts as a natural preservative and provides antioxidants benefits, protecting the skin from free radical damage.

Combine:

- 2 tablespoons Jojoba Oil
- 2 tablespoons Almond Oil
- 1 tablespoon Castor Oil
- 1 tablespoon Aloe Vera Gel
- 1 tablespoon Witch Hazel
- 5 drops Tea Tree Essential Oil
- 5 drops Lavender Essential Oil
- 5 drops vitamin E Oil

Instructions:

1. In a small bowl, combine the jojoba oil, almond oil, cad castor oil. Stir well to ensure they are thoroughly mixed
2. Add the aloe vera gel and witch hazel to the oil mixture. Stir thoroughly to combine all the ingredients.
3. Add the tea tree essential oil, lavender essential oil and vitamin E oil to the mixture. Stir well.
4. Transfer the mixture to a clean bottle/jar. Shake well before each use to ensure all ingredients are well

mixed.

5. Dispense a small amount on to a cotton pad or reusable makeup cloth remover.
6. Gently wipe the cotton pad over your face to remove the makeup.
7. For stubborn make up, hold the cotton pad over the area for a few seconds to allow the oils to break down the makeup.
8. Follow with your regular facial cleanser if you prefer a double cleansing routine.

29.Coco and Cinnamon foundation powder

Ingredients:

- Arrowroot Powder
- Cocoa Powder
- Bentonite Clay
- Ground Cinnamon
- Ground Nutmeg
- Lavender Essential Oil

Benefits:

Arrowroot Powder: provides a smooth, silky texture and helps to absorb excess oil, keeping your skin matte.

Cocoa Powder: adds natural color to the foundation to match your skin tone.

Bentonite Clay: adds coverage and helps to control oil, giving the foundation a matte finish and providing detoxifying benefits.

Ground Cinnamon: adds warmth to the foundation color and has antibacterial properties, which can help with acne prone skin.

Ground Nutmeg: provides a slight tint and has anti-inflammatory properties, which can help soothe the skin.

Lavender Essential Oil: Adds a pleasant scent and has soothing properties, making it ideal for sensitive skin.
Combine:

- 2 tablespoons Arrowroot Powder
- 1 tablespoon Cocoa Powder
- 1 tablespoon Bentonite Clay
- ½ teaspoon Ground Cinnamon
- ½ teaspoon Ground Nutmeg
- 5 drops Lavender Essential Oil

Instructions:

1. In a mixing bowl, combine the arrowroot powder and bentonite clay; mix thoroughly.
2. Gradually add the cocoa powder. Continue adding cocoa powder until you reach a shade that matches your skin tone.
3. If your skin has warm undertones, add a pinch of ground cinnamon to the mixture. For additional warmth or a deeper shade, add ground nutmeg in small increments.
4. Add lavender essential oil if adding to the mixture. This will give a pleasant scent and provide soothing properties.
5. Test the shade on your jawline or the back of your hand to ensure it matches your skin tone. Adjust the color by adding more cocoa powder, cinnamon or nutmeg as needed; mix thoroughly after each addition.

6. Shift the powder through a fine mesh sieve to remove any clumps and ensure an even consistency.
7. Transfer to a clean container/jar. Make sure to label and date. Store in a cool place.
8. If you use a primer, apply it before the foundation is applied.
9. Using a clean makeup brush or powder puff, dip into the foundation powder and tap off any access.
10. Apply the powder to your face in light, circular motions, starting from the center and working your way outward. Build coverage as needed by applying additional layers.
11. Spray your face with a natural setting spray or a mist of rose water to set the foundation.

Adjust their ratios to perfectly match your skin tone and type. You can experiment with other natural colorants like turmeric for warm undertones or activated charcoal for deeper shades.

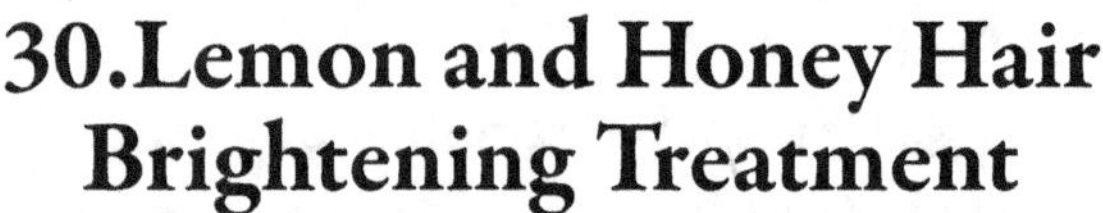

30. Lemon and Honey Hair Brightening Treatment

I*ngredients:*

- ½ Lemon Juice
- ¼ Chamomile Tea
- 1 tablespoon Honey
- 1 tablespoon Olive Oil
- Teaspoon Cinnamon Powder
- 1 tablespoon Apple Cider Vinegar

Benefits:

Lemon Juice: contains citric acid, which helps naturally lighten hair when exposed to sunlight.

Chamomile Tea: enhanced golden tones and provides a gentle, natural lightening effect.

Honey: acts as a natural humectant, drawing moisture into hair, and has mild lightening properties

Olive Oil: deeply moisturizes and conditions the hair, protecting it from drying out during the lightning process.

Cinnamon Powder: adds warmth to the hair color and enhances the lightning effect.

Apple Cider Vinegar: balances the scalp's pH, adds shine to the hair, and helps to remove buildup.

ECO-CHIC BEAUTY: A GUIDE TO DIY SELF-CARE

Combine:

- ½ cup Lemon Juice
- ¼ cup Chamomile Tea
- 1 tablespoon Honey
- 1 tablespoon Olive Oil
- 1 teaspoon Cinnamon Powder
- 1 tablespoon Apple Cider Vinegar

Instructions:

1. Brew 2-3 chamomile tea bags in ¼ cup of boiling water. Let it steep for 10 minutes, remove tea bags and let cool.
2. In a small bowl, combine lemon juice, cooled chamomile tea, honey, olive oil, cinnamon powder and apple cider vinegar. Stir well.
3. Pour into a clean spray bottle. Shake well before each use.
4. Apply treatment to clean, damp hair.
5. Shake the bottle well and spray the mixture evenly on hair, focusing on areas you want to brighten.
6. Use a wide-tooth comb to distribute the mixture evenly throughout your hair, ensuring that all strands are coated.
7. For more pronounced lightning effects, spend some time in the sun after applying the mixture. The UV rays from the sun help to activate the highlighting properties of the lemon juice and chamomile tea. Aim for 30 minutes to 1 hour of sun exposure.

8. Allow the mixture to sit for at least 1-2 hours. For a more intense effect, leave it on for 4 hours or even overnight. Use a shower cap if leaving overnight.
9. Rinse the mixture out of your hair thoroughly with lukewarm water. Follow up with a deep conditioner or a hair mask to restore moisture.

About the Author:

Raised in the vibrant and picturesque city of Vancouver, British Columbia, Mia Mirk developed an early affinity for the natural beauty surrounded her. Mia's childhood was spent exploring the lush forests, hiking the rugged mountains trails, and learning the delicate balance of the ecosystems that thrived in her backyard.

From a young age, Mia was captivated by the stories and recipes handed down through generations. Her grandmother's handwritten notes, wisdom regarding herbs and natural concoctions became a treasure trove of knowledge that Mia holds dear. These traditional recipes are woven into the fabric of her daily life, whether it's a soothing lavender balm for her children or a revitalizing tea blend to start the day. However, Mia's curiosity doesn't end with the old. She is a relentless explorer, always seeking out new natural products and innovative recipes to incorporate into her family's everyday life. Her kitchen often transforms into a bustling lab, where she experiments with fresh ingredients and sustainable practices. Mia's home is a lively sanctuary filled with laughter and the energy of her three kids, her supportive husband and their loyal big-hearted pup. Amidst the hustle and bustle, Mia remains grounded in her quest to incorporate nature's gifts to her family's life. Her journey into the world of natural remedies and eco-friendly products began to enhance her family's well-being but has since blossomed into a lifelong mission. From homemade skincare solutions to nutrient packed meals, Mia's creations are a testament to her belief in the healing power of nature. Mia has worked in the healthcare industry for over a decade, which has allowed her to seamlessly integrate natural remedies with modern medical practices.

Mia Mirk's life is a harmonious blend of care, tradition and innovation.

Don't miss out!

Visit the website below and you can sign up to receive emails whenever Mia Mirk publishes a new book. There's no charge and no obligation.

https://books2read.com/r/B-A-LFAJC-RLFXE

BOOKS 2 READ

Connecting independent readers to independent writers.

www.ingramcontent.com/pod-product-compliance
Lightning Source LLC
Chambersburg PA
CBHW061339140726
47997CB00003B/1018